A WARM WINTER TAIL

by Carrie A. Pearson
illustrated by Christina Wald

How do humans keep warm in the winter, Mama?
Do they wrap their tails tight
'round their bodies just right
as heaters to chase out the chill?

No fur tail for draping,
for covering and caping;
their blankets are cotton and wool.

How do humans keep warm in the winter?
Do they dig in the mud,
their skin covered with crud,
'til sunshine warms up their thick shells?

No mud soak that's oozing,
no crud cloak for snoozing.
Their mud baths must wait until spring.

How do humans keep warm in the winter, Mama?
Do they fluff up their feathers
whatever the weather
and shiver to make their own heat?

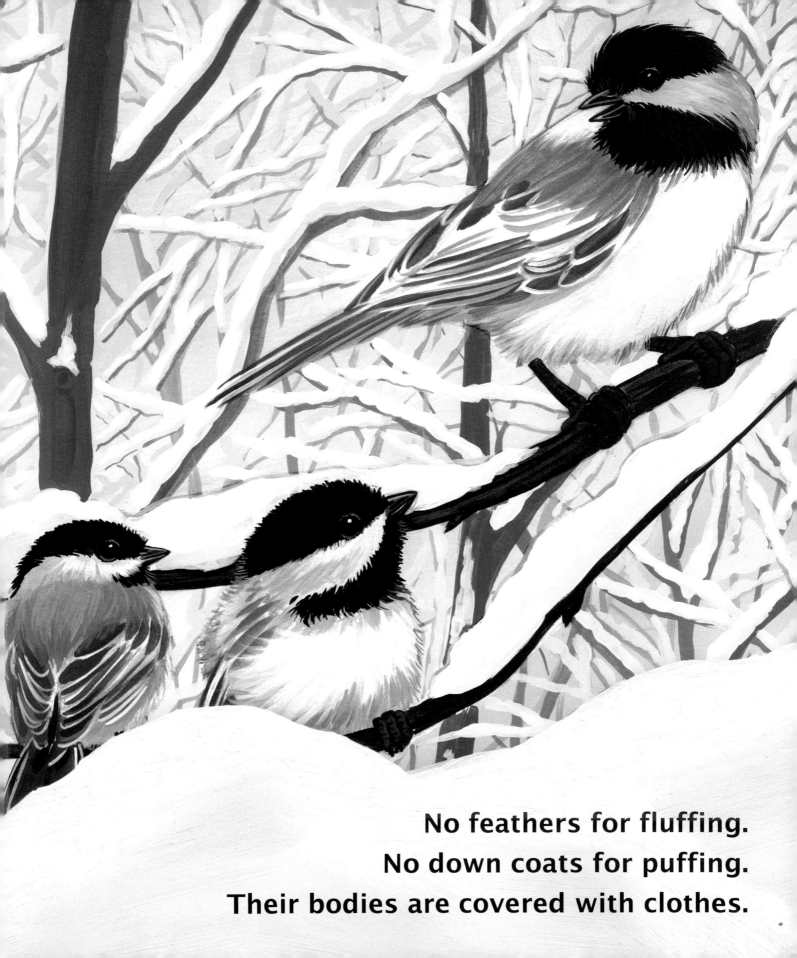

No feathers for fluffing.
No down coats for puffing.
Their bodies are covered with clothes.

How do humans keep warm in the winter, Mama?
Do they eat till they're plump,
go to sleep in a lump,
and wait for spring breezes to come?

No snoring and wheezing
while cold winds are teasing.
In winter, they're active all day.

How do humans keep warm in the winter, Mama?
Do they grow hollow hair
so the coats that they wear
trap the heat from their bodies for warmth?

No hair coats for warming
when winter is storming.
Their jackets have zippers and snaps.

How do humans stay warm in the winter?
Do they live in a bunch,
taking turns for their lunch
with Queen staying warm at the core?

No Queen in the center
where no one can enter.
Those humans don't live in a swarm.

How do humans keep warm in the winter, Mama?
Do they squeeze in aloft,
in dreys full and soft,
to share heat from their bodies with friends?

No nuzzling in tree nests
with room for a new guest.
They can't climb up a frost-bitten branch.

How do humans stay warm in the winter?
Is the sun their bright guide
as their wings fly and glide
to trees where it's warm all year long?

**No flying on strong wings
to flee what those winds bring.
They wish for the ice and snow!**

How do humans keep warm in the winter, Mama?
Do they skitter below,
through long tunnels of snow,
to hide from the wind and the cold?

No quick toes through snow.
They move much too slow
and their boots are too big for that trail.

How do humans stay warm in the winter?
Do their body parts freeze
hidden under some leaves
while winter goes on up above?

No body that's frozen.
That's not how they've chosen
to spend their long winters outside!

How do humans stay warm in the winter, Mama?
Do they soar low in the sky
all alone while they fly
many miles to a Mexican home?

No flying through skies.
No saying goodbyes.
Their arms are not made for that trip.

How do animals stay warm in the winter, Mama?
Do they bundle in clothes,
wrapping scarves 'round their nose
and pull on their boots and their gloves?

No covering with clothes,
no buttons or bows.
Their bodies know how to stay warm.

For Creative Minds

Animals and Winter Adaptation Fun Facts

Living things adapt to seasonal changes in different ways. Animals have adaptations to help them survive hot weather in the summer and cold weather in the winter. Even humans adapt to seasonal changes.

These adaptations can be changes in their bodies (physical) or they can be changes in things that the animals do (behavioral). Animals raised by a parent (or parents) learn some behaviors. Other animals never know their parents and survive purely on instinct. Can you tell which animals in the story could learn from their parents (say "mama") and which could not?

Many animals move to a different location (migrate) when the weather starts to get cold. They are following not only warmer weather and seeking shelter, but also are often following food sources. Birds are the most obvious migrators to most of us because they are so visible flying in huge flocks along bird "flyways" that run north to south. But not all birds migrate—some stay through cold weather if there are enough food sources. Some birds that don't migrate include cardinals, crows, sparrows, black-capped chickadees, hawks, and starlings. A few mammals (whales) and insects (Monarch butterflies) migrate. Even some grandparents migrate by spending the winter in warmer climates and coming back in the spring as the weather warms and the snow melts.

Other animals go to sleep for long periods during the winter (hibernation in mammals or brumation in reptiles). These animals slow their systems down so they don't need as much energy: their hearts beat slower, they don't breathe as often, and sometimes their body temperatures even drop. These animals spend the whole winter like this. Some animals might go to sleep for several weeks (dormancy) but then wake up to go to the bathroom or get something to eat before going back to sleep again.

Animals need food for energy. Even animals that hibernate, brumate, or go dormant still need enough energy for their bodies to get oxygen and for their hearts to pump blood. Migrators need enough energy to fly, swim, or walk to where they are going. Animals that stay through the cold weather need enough energy to keep warm and to be able to get food.

Many animals eat enough food to build up a layer of fat before winter arrives. Their bodies burn this fat for energy when there's no other food. Bears going into hibernation will be fat but wake up thinner—after all, they haven't eaten anything for months. Migrating animals may eat little or no food as they travel.

Some animals save (cache) food. Humans might run to the grocery store to stock up on food if they know a big storm is coming. Squirrels gather nuts in the fall so they have something to eat in the winter when they might not be able to find nuts. Some animals (beavers and muskrats) even build their food supply into their dens!

The types of food that animals eat change with the seasons too. Foods that are readily available in the summer are not around in the winter. Animals that eat green leaves, berries, or small insects won't be able to find that type of food during the winter. They might eat tree bark or small rodents instead.

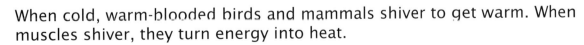

When it gets cold, humans heat buildings—schools, stores, and homes. The energy for that heat might come from electricity, gas, or oil. Just as we might try to save energy in our houses by turning down the temperature, some animals turn down their body temperatures to save food energy.

Humans wear thin jackets in the fall or spring but then wear heavy, warm coats in the winter. Many mammals grow thicker fur in the winter. Other mammals shed summer fur and grow winter fur. The winter fur is often two layers: an outer fur of hollow hairs to act as an insulator and a short, thick underfur. Fur colors might even change. The winter colors absorb and retain heat from the sun but the summer colors reflect the heat. Some birds molt summer feathers and grow thicker, warmer feathers for winter.

Many animals build or find warm winter homes to protect them from snow and wind. These homes can be underground, under rocks, under bushes, in piles of leaves, in tree hollows, or even dug right into snow! Some brumating reptiles or amphibians will even dig into mud at the bottom of a lake or pond!

Many animals will curl up to conserve body heat, just as we might curl up under warm blankets to stay warm. Animals cuddle with other animals—sharing body heat.

Some insects survive the long, cold winter as larva. When warm weather arrives, they move into the next stage of their life cycle. Other insects migrate long distances, and still others might find a warm spot and go dormant.

When cold, warm-blooded birds and mammals shiver to get warm. When muscles shiver, they turn energy into heat.

Tiny muscles attached to each hair make goose bumps. When the body is working to warm itself, these muscles raise the hairs for extra insulation. We don't have enough thick hair (fur) to make a big difference, but for mammals with thick fur, this helps a lot.

Winter Animal Matching Activity

box turtles

grey squirrels

black bears

white-tailed deer

honeybees

Black-capped chickadees

Match the animal to its description.

1 These small mammals build a sturdy nest, called a drey, and huddle together to take advantage of the body heat of others. They slow down their movements so they don't use as much energy and don't need a lot of their already stored food. They also grow a thicker coat of fur to trap more body heat.

2 These mammals eat and gain enough weight during the fall to have several inches of fat to provide enough energy during their long hibernation. While hibernating, their heartbeats drop from 40 to 50 beats a minute to only 8 to 12. Their temperature only drops a little, allowing them to wake up quickly if needed.

3 These reptiles brumate by burying themselves in up to two feet of mud, soil, or the remains of decaying plants. Some even move into mammal burrows to hide from cold weather.

4 These birds shiver to make body heat that is then trapped between their body and their fluffy down feathers. While they spend most of the day searching for food, at night they huddle together in sheltered areas to share body heat.

5 These mammals shed their fur in the spring and fall. Their summer fur is solid with no underfur. Their winter fur has two layers: a dark fur to absorb the sun's heat with hollow hair, and a thick underfur for extra insulation. They eat lots of food in the fall so they have a thick layer of fat. That fat provides almost half of the energy needed to survive the winter. When they get cold, they get goose bumps to raise fur for extra insulation.

6 These insects stay warm by clustering together inside their hive. The middle of the cluster, where the important queen and babies are kept, is about 80°F (26.6°C). The outside of the cluster is colder. They make heat by shivering and beating their wings. The animals on the outside move from the middle of the cluster to the outside and back again. They eat when they are on the outside of the cluster.

Answers: 1) grey squirrels, 2) black bears, 3) box turtles, 4) Black-capped chickadees, 5) white-tailed deer, 6) honeybees

and Animal Classes

Monarch butterflies

deer mice

humans

hummingbirds

wood frogs

red foxes

7 During the summer, these small mammals have plenty of vegetation to keep them hidden from predators. Winter snow protects them as they travel around in tunnels. Come spring, the grass will be indented where their tunnels ran under the snow. Adults can squeeze through openings that are no larger than a dime!

8 These mammals heat their homes and trap heat under warm clothing, blankets, coats, boots, mittens, and hats. Some retired adults even migrate to warmer climates for the winter.

9 These insects fly over 1500 miles (2400 km) to warm weather in Mexico or Southern California. Even though they are the "great-grandchildren" of the insects that made the same trip a year earlier, these animals even fly to the same trees! Scientists don't yet understand how they know where to go.

10 During the winter, these mammals curl into balls and wrap their tails around their noses and feet to stay warm. Sometimes they are completely covered with snow.

11 Even though they put on lots of weight before migrating, these birds need to eat often during their travels. They fly just over the treetops to easily catch insects and find nectar to drink. To hide from predators, they fly alone instead of in large flocks.

12 These amphibians are not great diggers so they hide in cracks of logs, old mouse burrows, or under leaf litter on the forest floor. When the temperature begins to drop, ice crystals form in almost half their bodies. A substance much like antifreeze in a car protects their hearts, lungs, and brains. They look like they are dried out and dead, but are really just suspended until warm weather thaws them again.

Match the colors to identify the animal classes. Which animals are mammals, reptiles, birds, insects, or amphibians?

Answers: 7) deer mice, 8) humans, 9) Monarch butterflies, 10) red foxes, 11) hummingbirds, 12) wood frogs
mammals: grey squirrels, black bears, white-tailed deer, deer mice, humans, and red foxes reptiles: painted turtles birds: Black-capped chickadees and hummingbirds insects: honeybees and Monarch butterflies amphibians: wood frogs

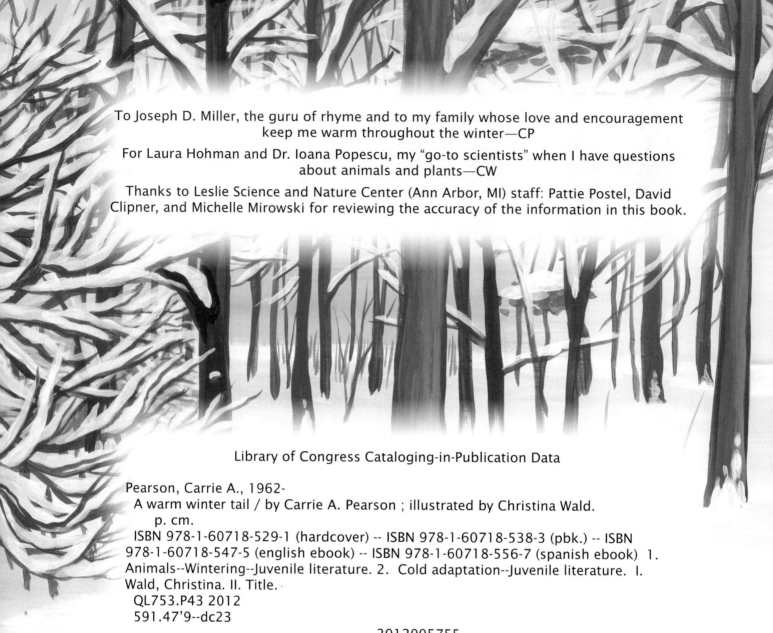

To Joseph D. Miller, the guru of rhyme and to my family whose love and encouragement keep me warm throughout the winter—CP

For Laura Hohman and Dr. Ioana Popescu, my "go-to scientists" when I have questions about animals and plants—CW

Thanks to Leslie Science and Nature Center (Ann Arbor, MI) staff: Pattie Postel, David Clipner, and Michelle Mirowski for reviewing the accuracy of the information in this book.

Library of Congress Cataloging-in-Publication Data

Pearson, Carrie A., 1962-
  A warm winter tail / by Carrie A. Pearson ; illustrated by Christina Wald.
    p. cm.
  ISBN 978-1-60718-529-1 (hardcover) -- ISBN 978-1-60718-538-3 (pbk.) -- ISBN
978-1-60718-547-5 (english ebook) -- ISBN 978-1-60718-556-7 (spanish ebook) 1.
Animals--Wintering--Juvenile literature. 2. Cold adaptation--Juvenile literature. I.
Wald, Christina. II. Title.
  QL753.P43 2012
  591.47'9--dc23

                              2012005755

Also available as an interactive read-aloud eBook featuring auto-flip, 3D-page-curling, and selectable English and Spanish text and audio (ISBN: 978-1-60718-566-6).

Hardcover Spanish translation: Un invierno muy abrigador (ISBN: 978-1-60718-680-9)

Interest level: 003-008   Grade level: P-3   Lexile® Level 730

key phrases for educators: adaptations, animal classes, anthropomorphic, compare/contrast, migration/hibernation, repeated lines, rhythm or rhyme, seasons (winter)

Manufactured in China, June, 2012
This product conforms to CPSIA 2008
First Printing

Sylvan Dell Publishing
Mt. Pleasant, SC 29464